This Journal Belongs To :

Made in the USA
Las Vegas, NV
11 June 2024

91007990R00069